A Lost Soul
Found in the Darkness:
The Journey of a Soul in Haiku

Brett C. Persson

A Lost Soul Found In The Darkness:

The Journey of a Soul in Haiku

HUMAN AUTHORED™
AG THE Authors Guild
1986635

brettcpersson@gmail.com
www.brettcpersson.com
X: @brettcpersson

Nudous Publishing, LLC

www.nudouspublishing.com
info@nudouspublishing.com

Paperback ISBN: 978-1-964793-76-4

Dedication

As I write this dedication, I draw strength from my higher power and use it to wish hope and healing upon those who suffer from addiction and abuse. Our world can be a cruel place, even for the ones who should love us unconditionally. I was fortunate to have two loving parents who supported and nurtured me as parents should; not everyone is as fortunate as I was.

My hope is that this book finds its way into the hands of those in need and brings just a little bit of comfort, strength, encouragement, and love. May it serve as a beacon of light leading them out of their darkness into brighter days filled with peace and joy. Let it also allow those who have never suffered from this affliction see a glimpse into the world of addiction.

Life can be difficult, especially when a person is struggling with addiction, abuse, or mental illness. We must never give up our pursuit of love and hope, for these are the antidotes to darkness. This book is dedicated to all those out there who find themselves or someone they love in the depths of despair - may it bring courage, compassion, and solace to their hearts.

Brett C. Persson

12/14/2022

Table of Contents

Childhood 1

The Teen Years 31

The Twenties 57

Trying Something New...77

Redemption And Salvation 89

The Years That Follow 105

Childhood

Jake Is Not Aware

Does Not Yet Remember Things

Still Leaves An Imprint

Left In Soiled Diapers

He Screams And Cries From The Pain

Rash Leading To Sores

Mom And Dad Fighting

Dad Striking Mom Till She Bleeds

Mom Throwing Dishes

Jake Hungry, Dirty

Neglected Most Of The Time

Little Food To Eat

Dad Is Watching Him

When Jake Cries Out, Dad Slaps Him

The Pain Leaves Its Mark

As Jake Grows, He Sees

Just A Toddler, But Aware

Regular Abuse

Sleep Interrupted

Sees The Lights Often At Night

Flashing Blue And Red

Confused What He Hears

Parents Screaming About Pigs

The Yelling Scares Him

Dad Is Taken Out

Mom Screams At Them As They Leave

Then Just Soft Sobbing

Dad Returns In Days

They Seem Happy Together

One Night Of Quiet

Drinking Quickly Starts

The Screaming Starts Soon After

Twisted Love And Hate

Jake Nearing School Age

Violence, Abuse Is Life

They Learn To Hide It

Mom Is Always Drunk

Dad Hits Where No One Can See

Jake Stays Clear Of Them

It Is The Old Ways

Police And Teachers Ignore

They Turn A Blind Eye

Jake Is Not Stupid

He Learns At A Steady Pace

Is Quiet And Shy

Jake Feels Safe At School

No Screaming And No Hitting

Fear And Hate At Home

Spills A Glass Of Milk

Dad Flicks Cigarette At Him

Jake Screams Loud In Fright

Embers Burn His Skin

Ash And Cherry Bounce Off Face

Jake Runs From Table

Mom Yelling At Dad

For Burning Her Baby Boy

Now She Seems To Care

Jake Cries In His Room

Worse Then Physically Hurt

Emotional Scar

Days Pass Peacefully

The Quiet Before The Storm

Jake Fears The Silence

Dad Laying On Floor

Glass And Blood Cover The Floor

Passed Out And Bleeding

Mom Steps Over Him

Looks At Him And Shakes Her Head

Spits On Him And Laughs

Jake At The Table

He Waits, Hopes For Some Breakfast

Mom Just Grabs A Beer

Jake Gets A Pop Tart

No Chance For Hot Meal Today

Just A Normal Day

Mom Drinks, And Dad Stirs

Jake Watches Morning Cartoons

Mom Is Drunk By Ten

Jake Getting Taller

Mom Throwing Him A Party

Turning Ten Today

Jake Is Excited

Cousins Are Coming Today

Hopes For A Good Day

Dad's Brother Arrives

With His Wife And Two Children

It Starts Out So Good

Presents And A Cake

Mom And Dad Start To Drink More

Starting To Get Loud

Tension Fills The Air

Uncle Dave Getting Upset

He Does Not Approve

Dave Starts To Lecture

Dad Grows Angry And Obscene

Dave Backs Off Calms Down

Dad Soon Does The Same

Jake Admires His Uncle Dave

Wishing He Was Dad

Uncle Dave Calls Dad

Dad Does Not Answer The Phone

He Just Ignores It

People At The Door

Asking About Jake's Safety

His Parents Tell Lies

Two People Sit Down

They Ask Jake Pointed Questions

Jake Lies Out Of Fear

The People Take Notes

Jake Wishes He Was Stronger

Too Scared To Speak Out

The People Soon Leave

Dad Is Pissed, Mom Is Upset

Dad Blames Uncle Dave

Dad And Mom Drinking

Dad Begins Smoking Something

Mom Slumped On The Couch

Jake Hides In His Room

There Is Noise Of Things Breaking

Jake Unsure Of What

Soon Those Lights Return

The Ones That Are Blue And Red

Pounding At The Door

Dad Yelling At Them

Louder Pounding And Shouting

There Is A Loud Crash

Splintering Of Wood

There Is A Large Commotion

Loud Swearing And Screams

Jake Knows This Is Bad

Sounds Of A Stick Hitting Meat

A Deafening Thud

A Sudden Silence

Sirens Come From A Distance

Growing Closer Still

Radios Chatter

More People Come To The House

Different Commotion

Jake Peaks Out The Door

People Stand Around Jake's Dad

Dad Bleeding And Bruised

Dad Is Not Moving

Someone Brings In A Stretcher

They Place Him On It

Mom Sitting On Couch

A Policeman Is Injured

They Ask Mom Questions

Mom Upset, But Calm

Hours Have Now Passed When They Leave

Mom Lays Down And Sleeps

Days Pass, Dad Still Gone

Mom Is Drinking Heavier

Jake Is All Alone

The Verdict Is In

Mom Tells Jake He Got Ten Years

Assaulting Two Cops

Jake And Mom Alone

Jake Is Neglected More Now

Jake Does Not Miss Dad

Jake's Is Turning Twelve

He Wants Uncle Dave To Come

Mom Says He Cannot

Jake Invites Some Friends

Mom Has Cupcakes For Them All

They Have Fun Playing

Mom Is Still Drinking

Jake's Friends Plan To Spend The Night

Mom Orders Pizza

The Kids Watch Movies

Mom Takes Her Bottle To Bed

She Closes Her Door

Now Almost Midnight

Jake And Friends Take A Bottle

Mom Will Not Miss It

The Label Says Gin

The Boys Sip On It And Gag

Jake Has His First Drink

The Taste Is Too Strong

Jake Mixes It With Some Juice

Is Much Better Now

Soon Jake Feels It Hit

Getting A Little Tipsy

Jake Feels The Gin's Gift

The Boys Drink Some More

They All Drink Some, Jake Drinks More

Jake Loves How He Feels

Head Spinning Around

Jake Has Never Felt Like This

Jake Has A New Friend

Jake Wakes Up, Head Hurts

Looks Around The Empty House

Friends Already Left

Jake Takes Aspirin

It Is Noon; Jake Straightens Up

Mom Is Still Sleeping

Makes Toast And Sausage

Jake Recalls How Good He Felt

He Plans His Next Drink

Mom Is Working Late

Jake Drinks Some Of Mom's Vodka

Better Than The Gin

Jake Drinks Way Too Much

Sick and Nauseous, He Throws Up

Mom Comes Home And Sees

Jake Feels Much Better

Mom Tells Him It Is Okay

All About Pacing

They Eat Some Pizza

They Share A Drink Together

Mom's New Drinking Friend

Some New Rules In Place

Only Allowed To Drink Beer

Jake Agrees To Rules

Jake Learns To Like Beer

Mom Gives A Six Pack A Day

She Drinks The Hard Stuff

Times Are Better Now

Jake And Mom Getting Along

Drunk Drinking Buddies

Celebration Time

Both Drink Extremely Heavy

Jake's Thirteenth Birthday

Jake Blacks Out Early

Mom Continues To Drink More

The Night Stretches On

Jake Wakes Up Still Drunk

Sees Mom Crumpled On The Floor

Something Different

Jake Goes To Her Side

Her Eyes Are Open And Blank

He Moves Back From Her

Jake Just Stares At Her

He Is Paralyzed With Fear

He Dials For Help

Paramedics Come

They Arrive And Check On Her

Jake's Mother Is Dead

Jake Struggles For Words

They Call For Social Worker

Jake Is All Alone

The Teen Years

Jake In A Group Home

He Goes To Mom's Funeral

Jake Only One There

Eight Teens In Each Room

Like A Prison Or Bootcamp

State Facility

Three Hots And A Cot

Kids Make Fun Of Him At School

Jake Starts Many Fights

Jake Steals Alcohol

Jake Still Drinks Almost Daily

Stays Out After School

Police Bring Him Back

Counselors Try To Reach Him

Jake Is Resistant

Jake Causing Problems

He Is Attacked While Sleeping

Pissed Off The Wrong Kid

Jake Gets The Kid Back

He Beats The Other Kid Bad

Broken Nose And Arm

Jake Told To Shape Up

Fly Right Or Go To Juvie

Hate And Anger Build

Jake Contains His Rage

He Acts The Way He Needs Too

Avoiding Juvie

Jake Hangs At Corner

The Older Boys Take Him In

A Bad Influence

Jake Begins Smoking

Drinking Continues To Grow

Reckless Abandon

Jake Is Now Fourteen

Steals A Car To Celebrate

A Joyride Through Town

Speeding Down The Street

Drunk And Car Out Of Control

He Takes A Turn Fast

Skids Out Of Control

Car And Telephone Pole Meet

Sound Is Horrific

Jake's Friend Dies At Scene

Car A Mangled Mess Of Steel

Jake Is Airlifted

Jake Fights For His Life

Over A Hundred Stitches

Seven Broken Bones

Months In Hospital

Jake's Recovery Is Slow

Plenty Of Pain Meds

Left Side Of Face Scarred

Now In Different Group Home

Still In Chronic Pain

Doctors Stop Pain Meds

Jake Turns To The Streets For Pills

Jake Steals For Money

Jake Young For Trial

Does Community Service

Jake Feels No Remorse

Works Out With A Friend

Jake Trying To Heal His Wounds

Rebuilding Muscle

Jake Often Truant

Group Home Lacks Supervision

Jake Sneaks Out Often

Drinks To Ease His Pain

Does Drugs When Available

Jake Gets What He Wants

Jake Is Now Fifteen

Smarter Than Most Around Him

Is Charismatic

Jake Fights When Needed

He Make Friends The Other Times

Jake Is No Victim

Jake Makes His Way Clear

His Years Of Abuse Payoff

His Dad Taught Him Well

Jake Looking Forward

Violence All He Has Known

Normal Part Of Life

Jake Perceived Older

He Continues To Workout

Stronger Than Ever

Still Using The Drugs

Pain From Accident Is Gone

Now Just To Get High

Caught Without Notice

Unknowingly Imprisoned

Drugs Taking Their Hold

Jake Does Well In School

He Misses Lots Of Classes

Teachers Shake Their Head

Jake Wastes Potential

His Teachers Try To Reach Him

Jake Will Not Listen

Crimes Are Increasing

Jake Breaking Into Houses

Hits Cars Late At Night

Jake Noticing Girls

Girls Notice Jake Even More

Hooks Up With Many

Many Girls Willing

Jake Tosses The Girls Aside

Nothing Is Long Term

Jake Shuts People Out

Will Not Let Emotion Build

Everyone Distant

Jake Getting Older

Takes Driving Test In Friend's Car

Passes Test With Ease

Jake Selling Drugs More

Saving Up For A Used Car

He Gets One Quickly

Jake Does Not Drive Drunk

Not Risking Himself Again

A Lesson Was Learned

Jake Has Many 'Friends'

Just A Few Real Close Friends

Jake Trusts None Of Them

Jake Sees Uncle Dave

Walking To The Corner Store

Shakes His Head And Laughs

Things Changing In Life

Jakes Closest Friend Leaves Group Home

Kicked Out Now Eighteen

Jake's Time Will Be Soon

A Year Away From Freedom

Finally Released

Jake Gets In A Fight

Alone On The Streets One Night

Two Men Against One

Jake Beaten Badly

Left In Side Alley Bleeding

Man Approaches Him

The Priest Helps Him Up

Takes Jake To His Church Nearby

He Tenders First Aid

Jake Is Reluctant

He Allows The Priest To Help

Sees No Other Choice

The Priest Makes Small Talk

Jake Tells Him More Than He Planned

He Listens To Jake

Time For Jake To Go

Bandaged And Feeling Better

Jake Thanks The Young Priest

The Priest Offers Help

Tells About God's Forgiveness

About Hope And Love

Jake Puts Up His Hand

He Politely Stops The Priest

Cannot Save Garbage

Priest Tries To Object

Jake Stops Him Again And Leaves

The Priest Is Distraught

Jake Thinks As He Walks

He Knows That The Priest Is Wrong

He Is Not Worth It

Jake Heals From The Fight

Not His First Time Being Beat

Life Is A Beating

Jake Now Has Freedom

He Is Released From State Care

His Life Begins Now

Moves In With A Friend

A Small Dirty Apartment

Pays His Share Of Rent

Gets Clothes From Steeling

Jake Sells Drugs For Rent And Gas

Is Living His Life

Jake And Roommate Drink

Lots Of Wild Parties And Girls

Jake Meets Stacy Lee

Jake Feels Different

She Has A Similar Past

They Bond And Connect

Stacy Stays Over

Jake Guesses That It Is Love

Two Peas In A Pod

Sometimes They Argue

Stacy Throws Things, Jake Hits Her

They Make Up With Sex

They Are Both Toxic

Feeding Each Other More Hate

Disguised As Young Love

Professing Their Love

Both Growing More Violent

Abuse Continues

The Good Times Are Great

Jake And Stacy Embrace Them

Ignore The Bad Times

Living Together

Sharing Their Lifelong Damage

Unshakably Bound

Living Life In Chaos

Feeding Off Of Each Other

Codependency

Doing What They Can

They Struggle To Make Ends Meet

Trying To Survive

The Twenties

Stacy Looking Thin
Celebrates Another Year
Still Bound Together

Jake Still On The Edge
Stacy Talks About Quitting
Jake Keeping Her Hooked

Stacy Tries To Quit
Jake Continues To Offer
She Cannot Resist

Stacy Is Concerned

Jake Says They Are In Control

Just Having Some Fun

Stacy Goes Along

She Loves Jake And She Trusts Him

Of Course, He Is Right

They Try Something New

They Start To Shoot Heroin

Feeling It Rush In

They Drink, Shoot, Party

Days Go By Without Notice

Jake Makes Her Feel Good

Stacy Still Worries

Jake Keeps Bringing In Money

She Wonders Where From

Jake Protects Stacy

Still Fight, Sometimes Violent

But Always Make Up

They Throw Huge Party

Police Arrive At Midnight

The Next-Door Neighbors

Jake Slurring Badly

The Police Grow Impatient

Stacy Intervenes

Complies With Police

Thanks Them For Understanding

Problem Adverted

Jake Comes Home Bloody

Cut Above Eye And On Lip

Knuckles Bruised And Raw

Stacy Cleans Him Up

Jake Has No Explanation

She Does Not Press Him

Stacy Takes A Test

She Fears She Knows Already

Positive, Pregnant

Stacy Is Worried

She Tells Jake She Is Pregnant

Jake Is Overjoyed

Stacy Stops Using

She Embraces This New Life

Jake Continues On

Stacy Is Steadfast

Avoids Drugs And Alcohol

Jake Is Supportive

Jake Still Partying
She Tries To Get Him To Stop
He Does Not Listen

They Fight About Drugs
Jake Still Refuses To Stop
The Argument Grows

Jake Slaps Stacy, Hard
Searing Pain Fills Stacy's Face
She Hides In Corner

Jake Is So Angry

She Is Scared For Her Baby

Sober, She Sees Him

Jake Shoots Up Heavy

Stacy Seeing With Clear Eyes

Jake Soon Passes Out

Stacy Gets Her Things

She Packs Two Bags Of Clothing

She Walks Out The Door

Jake Gets Out Of Bed

Notices Stacy Is Gone

Must Be At The Store

Hours Have Passed Him By

Jake Grows Worried About Her

He Goes To The Store

Jake Cannot Find Her

He Is Worried About Her

He Shoots Up And Waits

Days Go By, While High

Gets A Letter On Day Eight

Sorry And Goodbye

The Letter Hurts Him

Stacy Tells Him She Is Fine

She Cannot Trust Him

Living With Parents

Rebuilding Relationship

They Are Helping Her

No Way To Reach Her

Thought Her Family Was Gone

He Is Frustrated

Jake's Hate For Her Grows

Months Of Drug Use Building Hate

Resents Her Leaving

Stacy Should Have Stayed

Jake Knows It Was Not His Fault

It Is All Her Fault

Jake Using Heavy

Trying To Kill All The Pain

Finding No Relief

Jake Starts To Move On

Hooking Up With Random Girls

Love The One You're With

Months Passed Since She Left

Jake Knows His Child Has Been Born

Wonders, Boy Or Girl

Jake Stopped While Speeding

Cocaine And Heroin Found

Jake Is Arrested

Public Defender

Several Charges Pending

Explains Jake's Options

Jake Facing Six Years

Attorney Suggests A Deal

Jake Just Nods His Head

They Ask For Three Years

District Attorney Agrees

Must Attend Meetings

Jake Enters Prison

He Quickly Gets A Routine

Looks For A Hookup

Drugs Not Consistent

Jake Has Limited Money

Finds Some Alcohol

Jake Attends Meetings

Narcotics Anonymous

Jake Does Not Listen

Part Of His Sentence

Jake Blinded By Addiction

Is In Denial

Mandated Meetings

Jake Attends Three Times A Week

Just Sits In Silence

Three Months Pass Him By

Gets High Or Drunk When He Can

He Avoids Trouble

Group Led By Steven

Stops Jake After A Meeting

Jake Is Dismissive

Steven Tries Often

He Tries To Help Jake See Truth

Jake Keeps Resisting

Jake Is Desperate

He Steals Drugs From Wrong Inmate

He Is Beaten Down

Jake Left Badly Beat

Jake Left Fighting For His Life

Doctors Work On Him

Trying
Something New

Jake Wakes Up Confused

Unsure Of His Surroundings

Steven Sits Near By

Jake Knows Who He Is

Steven Explains What Happened

It Has Been Four Days

Steven Talks With Him

Actually Listening

Steven Tells His Path

Steven Clean For Years

He Shares His Story With Jake

A Similar Path

Jake's Mind Opening

Realizes He Needs Help

He Wants To Get Clean

Steven Teaches Jake

Twelve Steps Of Recovery

Jake Embraces Them

Jake Feels A Freedom

He Feels Something Different

Unsure But Hopeful

Jake Asks Him Questions

Talks About Higher Power

Jake Not Religious

Steven Explains It

Something Bigger Than Himself

A Higher Power

Jake Getting It Now

God Of His Understanding

Mind Starting To Clear

Jake Working The Steps

Fearless Reflection Of Self

Embraces Step Four

Sees It Clearly Now

Past Becomes Reality

Shame And Guilt Surface

Emotions Come Through

Steven Helps Jake Work Through It

A Heavy Burdon

Jake Filled With Regret

Steven Teaches Jake To Cope

Let Go and Let God

Jake Starts To Feel Peace

A New Unknown Clarity

Jake Sees Light And Hope

Gets Ninety Days Clean

Works The Program With Vigor

Talks And Shares His Fears

Progresses Through Steps

Jake Trying To Make Amends

Writes Deep Long Letters

One Day At A Time

Progress Over Perfection

Words Of Truth For Jake

Gold, Then Red, Then Blue

Jake Reaches Six Months Sober

Now Clean And Serene

Jake Is Feeling Good

Steven Warns Of Relapsing

Staying Vigilant

Jake Serves His Time Well

Works With Steven And Others

Addicts Help Addicts

Jake Has Two Years Clean

His Release Date Approaching

Deep Fear Builds Within

Steven Helps Fight Fear

Told To Trust Higher Power

Jake Anxious And Scared

Five Days To Release

Jake Unsure Of Where To Go

Worries Of Old Friends

Steven Offers Help

Jake Renting Room From Steven

A Good Stepping Stone

Walks Out A Free Man

Jake Takes In The Sun And Air

New Chapter In Life

Steven Takes Jake Home

Introduces Him To Wife

She Welcomes Him In

Jake Sees His New Place

A One Room Efficiency

Separate Entrance

Table, Bed, And Couch

A Clean Tile Floor And Plain Walls

A Nice Kitchenette

Redemption
And Salvation

Jake Works Construction

Enjoys The Physical Work

A Friend Of Steven

Jake Finds A Home Group

Has Gotten Close To Steven

Feels Like Family

Jake Thinks Of Stacy

Wonders What His Child Is Like

Maybe Meet Someday

Jake Goes To Meeting

Steven's Achieves Ten Years Clean

Meets Stevens Brother

He Looks Familiar

Steven's Brother Offers Hand

Jake Confused But Shakes

So We Meet Again

He Introduces Himself

Father Addison

It Takes A Moment

Jake Now Remembers The Priest

The Priest That Helped Him

Jake Is Stunned By It

Coincidence Or God's Work

Jake Feels Something Click

Starts Going To Church

Jake Learning About God's Love

The Priest Counsels Him

Feeling Not Worthy

Self-Loathing And Remorseful

Unworthy Of Love

Living With Regret

Jake Struggles With Forgiveness

Living With The Past

Fighting His Demons

Trying To Accept Jesus

His Heart Is Hardened

Trying To Believe

His Self-Doubt Holding Him Back

Trying To Be Free

Goes Through The Motions

Pain Of The Past Still Binding

Feels Undeserving

Father Teaches Him

God's Grace And Love Will Heal All

Jesus Still Loves Him

Jake Prays For God's Help

Jake Striving To Move Forward

Starts To Feel God's Grace

Learning To Let Go

Jake Can Forgive His Parents

Feels Some Peace At Last

Continues To Learn

Jake Decides To Get Baptized

Emotions Flood In

Surprised By Feelings

Feels God's Grace Wash Over Him

Embraced By His Love

Jake Works His Program

Giving Back What He Received

Jake Shares His Story

Jake Joins H. And I.

Hospitals, Institutions

Addicts In Prison

Sharing Hope And Love

Helping Others Recover

Sober And Happy

Jake Rebuilding Life

Finally Moving Forward

Forgetting Regret

Opens Cold Shelter

Jake Helps Father Addison

Doing Ministry

Jake Feeling Alive

Trusts In God's Plan For His Life

Knows Jesus Saved Him

A Three-Year Journey

Building A Relationship

Coming To God's Love

Faith In Jesus Christ

Accepts Jesus As Savior

Repents For His Sins

Confirmed In The Church

Soul Still Damaged, But Mending

God's Healing Love Felt

Humbled By His Grace

Endless Possibilities

Everlasting Life

Jake Reflects On Life

So Many Sins On Others

He Forgives Himself

Unburdens His Sins

Jake Confesses To The Lord

He Is Forgiven

Jake Extends Outreach

Helps Open A Soup Kitchen

Works With The Homeless

Helping Others Live

Helps His Own Sobriety

Giving His Support

Compassion And Love

Helping People Like He Was

Lost In The Darkness

Jake's Burden Released

Now Five Years Free From Prison

Found His Inner Peace

Jake Thinks Of His Child

He Has Come To Terms With It

Will Never Know Her

Jake Hopes She Is Safe

Prays For Her Health Everyday

Prays For Stacy Too

Filled With The Spirit

Life In God's Grace Has Been Good

Found His Salvation

The Years That Follow

Ten Years Since Prison

Jake Meets Peyton At The Church

Quickly Hit It Off

They Meet For Coffee

Share, Talk, And Listen For Hours

Time Swiftly Passes

Peyton Is Younger

Jake Seven Years Her Senior

Neither Seems To Care

She Tells Him Stories

Normal Happy Family

Jake Shares With Peyton

Peyton Cries For Him

Childhood She Cannot Picture

Neglect, Abuse, Hate

Jake Shares His Dark Past

He Tells Her About Stacey

Shares His Prison Life

Violence And Drugs

Loving The Way He Was Taught

Becoming His Dad

Peyton Feels For Him

Jake Shares His Recovery

Then Feeling God's Grace

Peyton And Jake Date

Taking It Slow, Not Rushing

Building Trust And Love

The Pray Together

Minister To The Homeless

Spreading God's True Love

Peyton Takes Him Home

Jake Meets Peyton's Family

They Welcome Him In

They Visit Often

Jake Bonds With Her Dad Brian

Her Mother Likes Jake

Jake Chairing Meetings

Helping Others To Get Clean

Living A Good Life

Jake Takes Peyton Out

Two Year Anniversary

Dinner And A Show

Jake Takes Peyton Home

Inside Jake Goes To A Knee

Black Box, Diamond Ring

Jake Tells Her Of Love

He Proposes To Peyton

She Cries And Accepts

A Short Engagement

Father Addison Presides

Beautiful Wedding

Honeymoon, Hatti

Helping Those In Need Rebuild

Missionary Work

Celebrating Love

Helping Others Receive God

Building A New Church

Peyton Gets Pregnant

Jake Is Happy And Thankful

Family Building

They Have A Daughter

Beautiful, Healthy, And Strong

They Name Her Sawyer

Together They Thrive

Jake Now A Drug Counselor

Giving Others Hope

Feeding And Housing

Peyton Helps In The Shelters

Sawyer Learns God's Word

Jake's Past Seems Distant

Feels Like A Lifetime Ago

His Life So Altered

Jake Thanks God Daily

Spreads God's Words Of Salvation

Bringing Out The Light

Service Calls Them Both

Peyton Starts Women's Shelter

Abused And Homeless

The Church Sponsors Them

They Help Hundreds Every Year

Saving Lives And Souls

Jake Turning Fifty

Sawyer Going To College

Peyton Proud Of Both

Private Gathering

Jake And Peyton Renew Vows

Sawyer Stands With Them

Father Addison

Steven, Her Parents, And Friend

Just Those That Are Close

The Years Carry On

Peyton And Jake Intertwined

Two Souls Joined As One

Helping The Others

Jake Still Making His Amends

Redeeming His Past

Jake Doing His Part

Letting God's Love Do The Rest

Jake Is The Servant

Sawyer Gets Married

Peyton And Jake Are Joyful

She Shares God's Message

As Jake Turns Sixty

His Grandson Jacob Is Born

Family Growing

1. Peyton Parent's Pass

Sad But Knows It Is God's Plan

Age Catches Us All

Life Is Good For Them

Fulfilling And Meaningful

They Work And Worship

Jake Getting Older

Slowing Down As Time Goes On

Looks Back At His Life

Proud Of Who He Is

Finally Forgives Himself

Put Regrets To Rest

Jake Is Eighty-Three

He Now Has Three Grandchildren

Peyton His Soulmate

He Dreams Of His Life

It Slowly Ebbing Away

Drifting In Deeper

Enveloped In Love

Jake Feels God's Warming Embrace

The Kingdom Awaits

Life Started Out Hard

Troubled And Filled With Darkness

The Journey Was Long

Road To Salvation

Worth The Struggle And The Pain

God's Plan Is Fulfilled

ABOUT THE AUTHOR

Born in 1973, Brett C Persson is a poet and recovering alcoholic who crafts his experiences into thought-provoking poetry and prose. As the author of his debut book, "Poetry Of An Addict" and several other collections, Brett hopes to provide readers with poignant insights into the life of a recovering addict as he ranges across universal themes through descriptive wordplay and vivid imagery. He aims to reassure readers who are struggling with alcoholism that they're not alone, helping them find solace in the unique and expressive power of poetry. Brett currently resides in Buckeye, Arizona with his wonderful wife and three daughters.

11/14/11

www.ingramcontent.com/pod-product-compliance
Lightning Source LLC
Chambersburg PA
CBHW052148170626
46812CB00004B/1638